BY J. L. SMITH

The Abominators

The Abominators in the Wild

The Abominators and the Forces of Evil

The ABOMINATORS

And my AMAZING Panty Wanty Woos!

J. L. SMITH

ILLUSTRATED BY SAM HEARN

www.littlebrown.co.uk

LITTLE, BROWN BOOKS FOR YOUNG READERS

First published in Great Britain in 2013 by Little, Brown Books for Young Readers
Reprinted 2013 (twice), 2014 (three times)

A CIP catalogue record for this book
is available from the British Library.

ISBN 978-1-907411-62-5

Typeset in Golden Cockerill by M Rules
Printed and bound in Great Britain by
Clays Ltd, St Ives plc

Papers used by LBYR are from well-managed forests
and other responsible sources.

MIX
Paper from
responsible sources
FSC FSC® C104740
www.fsc.org

Little, Brown Books for Young Readers
An imprint of
Little, Brown Book Group
100 Victoria Embankment
London EC4Y 0DY

An Hachette UK Company
www.hachette.co.uk

www.littlebrown.co.uk

For Russ, Josh, Ben and Angus

It was break time at Grimely East Primary School, on a warm summer's day. The sun was shining. End of term and the long summer holidays were just a few weeks away. Happy in the sunshine, children ran, skipped and hopped across the playground.

But three children had no time for such foolish matters as running, skipping or hopping. They had more important things to think about.

They were members of the Abominators, the naughtiest children in Year 5.

"What's going on?" said the first. He had large, round ears, a twitchy nose and a pointed chin. These mousey features were why he was known as Cheesy. Although he looked very well behaved, with his neatly ironed shirt and his round glasses, Cheesy loved causing trouble. When he was only five he filled the school drinking fountain with worms.

"Dunno," said the second. This was Boogster, the smallest of the three, given his nickname because he could flick a bogey from one end of the classroom to the other. His other major skills were skateboarding and breakdancing. Boogster made up for being small by causing mayhem at every opportunity, like the time he hid a bucket of frogspawn in the staffroom. Which soon turned into five hundred tiny, leaping frogs.

"I'm bored. Where's Mucker got to?" complained the third, a tall, scowling girl. The fastest runner in the gang, she liked – mainly to annoy her mum – to be known as Bob. Leaning against the bike shed with her hands in her pockets, she looked exactly like a boy apart from the long pigtail hanging down her back.

Bob earned her place in the Abominators by stink-bombing the entire school one parents' evening.

"Here he is!" said Cheesy.

Mucker, called this because he liked to muck around, made his way across the playground. He strolled casually with his hands in his pockets, kicking a stone in front of him.

Mucker was the leader, not because he was the biggest and strongest and could beat everybody at arm-wrestling (though he was, and he

4

could). And not because he had the loudest voice (though he did). He was the leader because, like all great leaders, he was the one with the best ideas.

It was Mucker who thought of filling the toilets with strawberry jelly.

It was Mucker who thought of hiding the gerbil in the school piano.

And it was Mucker who switched two serving trays one very memorable lunch time, so the dinner lady served sausage and ice cream … followed by apple pie and mashed potato.

Mucker, Cheesy, Bob and Boogster (otherwise known as the Abominators) were officially Grimely East Primary's most mischievous pupils. Their antics made the teachers say things like:

The gang were always getting into trouble. Even their form teacher Miss Jeffries, who was absolutely the nicest teacher in the school, got fed up with them.

"Can't you just concentrate and try to *learn* something?" she would say.

And they would try. Really. For about one

minute. But then Mucker would make a loud farting noise, or Cheesy would think of a rude joke, or Boogster would flick his bogey across the room and it would land on Miss Jeffries's head … and then they were in trouble. Again.

Mucker reached the rest of the gang, giving the stone a final kick, which sent it flying over the roof of the bike shed. The others watched in admiration.

"What are we doing?" asked Boogster.

"How should I know?" said Mucker. "Anyone got any ideas?"

"How about putting fake dog poo in the girls' changing room?" suggested Boogster.

"We done that last week," Mucker yawned.

"What about hiding the teacher's kettle?" said Cheesy.

"We can't do that, you numpty," said Bob. "They're still in there with it, aren't they? They're eating their Bourbon biscuits and custard creams and talking about what was on telly last night."

"Well, we could always do it later," Cheesy muttered.

"I know," said Bob, more gently this time, as she could see she'd offended Cheesy. "It's a good plan. But how about thinking big this time? Let's do a Major Operation!"

"We haven't done a Major Operation in a while," nodded Mucker, his eyes narrowing in thought, "not since we turned the lunch hall into a skating rink."

"Yeah," said Cheesy, wistfully, "who'd have thought we could make the floor so slippery with just a few bottles of vegetable oil. That was genius!"

"Pity Mr Nutter slipped and broke his leg," said Boogster.

"And his arm," remembered Cheesy.

"And his collarbone," added Mucker.

"He wasn't very happy, was he?" said Boogster.

"So what'll we do this time?" said Bob. "Come on, Mucker, you're the one with the ideas!"

"Major Operations are far too important to discuss in the open," said Mucker importantly, looking from left to right as if they might be being spied on. "They're probably watching us on CCTV, lip-reading us or something. Let's go to HQ."

Important gang discussions and meetings were always held at the Abominators' Top-Secret Gang Headquarters, otherwise known as the school storeroom. None of the teachers went there because it was dusty and cobwebby, full of old, discarded, forgotten and broken things that nobody needed. It was the gang's favourite place for:

mischief planning
burping competitions
homework copying
arm-wrestling competitions
eating smuggled-in crisps

They'd even done some graffiti on the wall. Boogster had written:

ABOMINATORS WOZ HERE

But he wrote it in pencil – in case they might need to rub it out for security reasons.

"Race you!" shouted Bob. "Last one there's a gibbering gibbon!"

The gang ran round the back of the school,

through a side door and down a corridor. But when they got to the storeroom it was – for the first time ever – not empty.

There were three people in the room.

The first person was the school secretary, Mrs Magpie, looking annoyed because she was getting covered in cobwebs. She was rummaging through an ancient cardboard box labelled "SECOND-HAND SCHOOL UNIFORM".

The second person was a tall man with the longest beard they had ever seen in their lives.

And the third person was a boy of their age. He was skinny, with blond hair neatly combed in a centre parting. And he was wearing a pair of bright pink silk pants with a gold embroidered crest on them.

"Children! Out of here *immediately*! This room is out of bounds!" trilled Mrs Magpie, waving a school polo shirt.

"If you will *excuse* me," added the boy, in the poshest voice the Abominators had ever heard, "I would like some privacy, please. I'm in nothing but my panty wanty woos!"

The Abominators left the storeroom.

They walked out into the playground.

They sat down by the football goals.

Never, in their lives, had they been lost for words. Until now.

*

For a long time they sat in silence, trying to make sense of what they had just seen. At last Mucker spoke.

"That was … strange!"

The others nodded.

"Weird!" added Cheesy.

"Do you think he'll be in our class?" Bob wondered.

"Hope not." Cheesy shook his head. "Did

you see his girls' pants? Who wears pants like that? And *what* did he call them?"

"He called them his 'Panty wanty woos' ... " said Mucker solemnly. Then he smiled, then he grinned, and then he gave a great big snort. Soon they were all laughing. They laughed and laughed and laughed, so hard their ribs hurt.

"Panty wanty woos!" repeated Boogster in wonder. "Would you believe it? Prancing about in girls' pants. What a dimmock!"

You may be wondering about the boy in the pink silk pants – and how he'd turned up at Grimely East Primary School. Well, to explain this we must go a few months back in time to a place called Trumpington Manor.

This was the home of Cecil Trumpington-Potts.

Cecil was brought up by a fearsome but kind nanny called Mabel Drudge who made sure that he had every luxury his father could afford. This included many pairs of silk pants in every colour of the rainbow, embroidered with the Trumpington-Potts family crest.

Mabel only ever talked to Cecil in baby talk. So his pants were his "panty wanty woos", his trousers were his "trousy wousys" and when he went to the toilet she would ask him if he had "made a wee wee" or "done a poo poo" or – occasionally – "gone to do potty". Cecil thought that this was a perfectly delightful way to talk.

Lord Trumpington-Potts spent most of his time travelling the world on a camel and only saw his son on birthdays and Christmases, when he would call him Cyril or Percy or – for some reason – Ralph.

Cecil had never, ever in his whole life been beyond the enormous grounds of Trumpington Manor. He didn't need to. There were lots of fun things for Cecil to do, like: collecting bugs, which he kept in elaborate bug mansions built out of matchsticks; swimming in the ornamental fountain; and wrestling his pet grizzly bear, Boris.

Because there was no school posh enough for him, Cecil was tutored by an absent-minded genius called Professor Zyloonsky, who taught him complicated and clever things like Einstein's Theory of Relativity, and how to outstare a panda.

One day Cecil was summoned to the library by his father, who stood solemnly by the fireplace and announced in his booming voice.

"Percy, we are ruined! The money is gone, every brass farthing of it!"

"Father, how can this be?" said Cecil.

Lord Trumpington-Potts looked embarrassed. The reason he was embarrassed was that it was his fault. He'd lost the family fortune because he had three giant weaknesses:

1. If he heard that it was anyone's birthday he would get them an enormous and very expensive present – even if he hardly knew them.

2. He spent a fortune on beard-grooming equipment and lotions.

3. He liked to invest his money in interesting schemes, which he was sure were bound to succeed. Such as ...

Baseball Caps for Sheep (why did nobody think of it before?)

Soup in a Hat (enjoy your lunch on the go!)

Super Pillow, the World's Comfiest Spy Pillow (with built-in nuclear bomb)

Robotic Dance Partner (ideal for all social events!)

Roller Sticks (for your more adventurous pensioner)

As he stood before his son, admitting that they were ruined, Lord Trumpington-Potts was surprised to notice that the boy was looking rather pleased.

*

After Lord Trumpington-Potts handed over the keys to the Trumpington Manor to the bailiffs, Cecil's nanny gave them a lift into the nearest town – which was called Grimely.

"Where will you go, dear and loyal Mrs Drudge?" asked Lord Trumpington-Potts.

"I'm going to sail the seven seas in my enormous luxury yacht," she replied, "the one you gave me for my birthday last year. I will miss you both, but you're too old for a nanny now, Cecil. And it's about time I saw the world. I'm off to have the adventure of my life!"

"Splendid. Have a good time," said Lord Trumpington-Potts, sadly.

And so father and son were left on a street

corner with nothing but some trunks full of toothbrushes and Lord Trumpington-Potts's collection of fancy clothes for every occasion – and of course Cecil's enormous assortment of panty wanty woos.

*

The staff at Grimely Job Centre were amazed at the sight of Lord Trumpington-Potts in his ruffled shirt and velvet breeches, his beard tied with a blue velvet ribbon, filling in forms with a giant peacock-feather quill-pen to say that he was available for work.

Under the Skills/Profession/Trade section, he wrote "NONE".

"That's not true, father!" protested Cecil. "You are very good at riding a camel, *and* giving presents *and* having the longest beard in England!"

Unfortunately, there were no jobs requiring

camel-riding or present-giving skills, or where having the longest beard in England was at all helpful.

*

A week later, Cecil and his father were living in a tiny bedsit, which smelt of cabbages. This was because the previous tenant was the World Cabbage-Eating Champion. A nice lady who lived next door helped them to settle in. Realising that they were clueless about how to look after themselves, she did her best to give them some useful pointers.

"This is how to make a cup of tea," she explained, making a cup of tea.

"This is how to make your beds," she explained, making Cecil's bed.

"This is how to clean your toilet," she explained, handing the toilet brush to Lord Trumpington-Potts, who turned a peculiar shade of green. He was so upset, his top hat tilted sideways.

That night, as they sat eating baked beans and radishes – which was all they could afford – Lord Trumpington-Potts cleared his throat.

"These are dark days, Cyril, the darkest days we've ever seen. We've hit rock bottom!

Tomorrow, you have to go to ... *Grimely East Primary School!"*

Long after his father was snoring through his impressive beard, Cecil lay wide awake, his eyes round and excited. At last he was going to school, which meant that for the first time in his life he was going to have friends. He could hardly wait.

"I'd like you all to meet the new boy!" said Miss Jeffries brightly. "His name is Cecil Trumpington-Potts. Welcome to the class, Cecil!"

Cecil stood beside Miss Jeffries and surveyed his new classmates with a happy, expectant smile. In the back row of the class he noticed four children with mischief shining out of their beady little eyes. The same children who'd burst in on him in the storeroom half an hour earlier.

Cecil very much liked the look of them. He liked the look of them so much, he decided that they would be his new friends.

I'd like you all to meet the new boy! His name is Cecil Trumpington-Potts.

"How's your panty wanty woos?" one of them shouted, and the whole class burst out laughing.

"No shouting in class!" scolded Miss Jeffries.

"They are extremely comfortable, thank you," said Cecil, smiling at the round-eared boy, "unlike these shorty wortys, which are rather tight."

The Abominators looked dumbfounded.

"Well, I'm sorry to hear your shorts are tight, Cecil," said Miss Jeffries. "Now would you take the spare seat in the back row? We're doing some reading this morning, so you might want to pick a book from the shelf over there."

Cecil took a book at random and sat down. Occasionally he peeked over the top of his book to watch his new friends (who did not yet know they were his friends). They were kicking and nudging each other, throwing paper aeroplanes and generally being noisy. This is exactly what

I've been missing all these years, Cecil thought to himself.

Boogster winked at Mucker.

"Watch this," he whispered, and threw his rubber at Cecil. It was a direct hit.

Cecil jumped to his feet, clutching his ear. Then he looked over and saw Boogster laughing. He smiled back in delight and gave him a "thumbs up" sign. Then he took off his shoe and threw it. It hit Boogster right between the eyes and knocked him out of his chair.

"Cecil!" cried Miss Jeffries, as she helped a dazed Boogster to his feet. "What on *earth* are you doing?"

"Making a friend," said Cecil, happily.

"Well I don't think that's how you're supposed to make friends," said Miss Jeffries.

Cecil noticed that his four friends-to-be were all glaring at him.

"I think you're right," said Cecil.

"Try to behave, Cecil," Miss Jeffries said.

Boogster caught Cecil's eye and, making a gun with his fingers and thumb, pretended to shoot him.

Cecil pretended to shoot back, and as the shoot-out continued, got more and more excited until he could not contain himself. He leapt to his feet.

"BANG! BANG! You're DEAD! You're DEAD! You're VERY VERY DEAD!" he squealed, jumping up and down.

"*Cecil!*" Miss Jeffries rushed over. "Would you please sit down and behave? First throwing shoes, and now this!"

"I'm sorry, Miss Jeffries," said Cecil, "I was being a cowboy from the Wild West."

"Well, please sit down and be quiet." Miss Jeffries was looking weary. "Are you enjoying your book?"

"I LOVE it!" said Cecil excitedly. "I've never read a book like this before. It seems to be about a boy called Charlie winning a golden ticket to go to a chocolate factory. I suspect that this will be a life-changing experience for him."

"So what do you usually read, Cecil?" asked Miss Jeffries.

"Well," said Cecil, "nothing as good as this. I've recently been reading Russian novels, in the original Russian language, of course. Professor Zyloonsky taught me five languages by the time I was six. Why are you staring at me with your mouthy wouthy open?"

Boogster nearly fell off his chair a second time, not because he'd been hit by another shoe, but because he was laughing.

"He just gets better and better!" cackled Cheesy, nudging Mucker in the ribs.

Cecil smiled across at the Abominators, pleased that they seemed to enjoy school so much. Near the end of the lesson, Miss Jeffries sent him to have his welcome talk with the school nurse.

"See you at din dins! I'm a hungry boy!" he said over his shoulder, as he left.

"Not if we see you first!" shouted Bob. And they dissolved into laughter again.

He didn't quite understand what they meant, but Cecil was sure that soon they'd be his best friends.

*

The head teacher of Grimely East Primary School, Mr Nutter, was sitting in his office, in a very bad mood about the Head Teachers' Conference on Monday.

He was going to have to share a room with the head teacher of Lofty Heights Primary up the hill, Mr Butter, a smug and annoying man who snored like a water buffalo.

Lofty Heights Primary was the school the children from the rich end of town went to. It had stained-glass windows and a mosaic floor in its entrance hall. It had double glazing, clean toilets and every other comfort you can imagine ... unlike Grimely East Primary, which was, to be honest, rather grotty.

When he wasn't keeping Mr Nutter awake with his ear-shattering snoring, Mr Butter enjoyed bragging to him about his school's

STRAIGHTEST
TIE
WINNER!
LOFTY HEIGHTS
PRIMARY.

successes – like winning the Grimelyshire Best Behaved Children Award, or the Straightest Tie Trophy.

If only, thought Mr Nutter, we could beat Lofty Heights Primary at something. *Anything.* I'd like to see that smug look wiped off Butter's face! I'd also like to see him pecked by a flock of insane budgies. That's what I'd like to see!

Mr Nutter's secret dark thoughts were interrupted at that moment by a knock on the door.

"Come in!" he barked.

It was Mr Coleman, the Year 6 teacher.

"Mr Nutter, I have to report an incident in

the lunch hall," said Mr Coleman, "involving those children in Year 5 and the new boy, Trumpington-Potts."

"Oh," Mr Nutter sighed, "what's happened?"

"I think, sir, you should come and see for yourself."

When he got to the lunch hall, Mr Nutter could not believe his eyes. Every child was covered from head to toe in chocolate flan. Every child except one. Clean as a whistle, and with not one single bit of flan on him, was Cecil Trumpington-Potts.

"Explain this!" shouted Mr Nutter.

Cecil got to his feet, and pointed at the

table next to him where the chocolate-coated Abominators were sitting, looking subdued.

"Well, sir, I overheard my new friends saying that it would be fun to have a food fight and I heard them say my name. So I organised one. It was a great success!"

"You *organised* one?" Mr Nutter could hardly get the words out. "And how on earth did you manage to stay so clean?"

"Well, my Nanny Drudgy always taught me not to get dirty – she said I should stay squeaky clean from my little nosie nose to my twinkle toes. So I hid under the table and shouted "FOOD FIGHT! FOOD FIGHT!" very loudly, until it was all over. I think my shouting really helped to encourage everyone, don't you?"

There was a loud snort from the Abominators.

"Detention for all five of you, after school!

You can clean up this mess!" barked Mr Nutter, turning and sweeping out of the lunch hall.

The Abominators groaned loudly, but Cecil was delighted.

"My very first detention!" he said happily, with a giant smile on his face.

*

Miss Jeffries was not in a good mood when she called the class to order after lunch, her hair still damp from washing out a bogey which had landed on her head that morning.

"I am *not* in a good mood!" she said. "There are some maths problems on your desks; see how far you can get with them in the next ten minutes, and then I'll go through them with you."

Mucker and his gang booed at the mention of the word "maths". Cheesy was making an elaborate spit ball. They all glared at Cecil, agreeing in whispers that they would "get" him in detention. Cecil sat and smiled his biggest smile, delighted to be back in the same class as his friends-to-be.

A few minutes later, not understanding that you are supposed to put your hand up, Cecil waved at Miss Jeffries.

"Yes, Cecil?"

"Well, there is a picture of three piggy wiggys. Then there is a 'minus' sign and a picture of *two* piggy wiggys and then there is an 'equals' sign."

"Yes," said Miss Jeffries. "Are you finding the sum too difficult?"

"No, Miss Jeffries," said Cecil. "As sums go, I shouldn't think you get much easier. What I have the problem with is why have you involved the poor ickle piggy wiggies? And *what's* happened to the two that you've taken away? Are you going to turn them into bacon sandwiches?

Excuse me, but your mouthy wouthy is hanging open again."

Mucker, Cheesy, Boogster and Bob tried not to laugh, but they could not help themselves. They guffawed, they sniggered and they chuckled away at the sight of the astounded Miss Jeffries.

"Well, Cecil," Miss Jeffries managed, when she recovered herself, "perhaps you would like to pick a book and read quietly instead?"

Cecil got up and fetched the book he'd been reading that morning.

"Back to the chocolate factory!" he said to nobody in particular. "This is SO MUCH better than Shakespeare!"

*

After school, Cecil went to the lunch hall to help clean up the food-fight mess. The Abominators were already there, holding buckets and mops and looking menacing. Boogster was looking particularly annoyed, perhaps because of the large bruise on his forehead from Cecil throwing his shoe at him earlier.

Mr Coleman was supervising. He was annoyed, because he'd been going to ask Miss Jeffries to go out for a coffee after school – the first part of his master plan to eventually marry her. Now instead of staring into her eyes over a cappuccino, he had to watch Cecil and the Abominators making a very bad job of mopping up chocolate flan.

"Don't throw so much water on the floor!" he shouted.

Mucker sidled up to Cecil. "Snitch!" he hissed.

Cecil grinned. "Is that going to be my nickname?" he said. "I quite like it. Or what about Snitchy Witchy?"

A little bit later Bob walked past Cecil and whispered, "Tattle Tale!"

Cecil looked confused. "Tattle Tale I'm not so keen on; it's not so catchy. No, I think we should stick with Snitchy Witchy."

Next Boogster deliberately bumped into him and out of the corner of his mouth said, "Grass!"

"Grass?" said Cecil. "Now that's just weird. I suppose it could be Snitchy Grass?"

Finally Cheesy spilled some water on Cecil's shoes. "Blabber mouth!"

"WHAT'S GOING ON?" Cecil threw down his mop. "Would you all PLEASE make up your minds what my nickname's going to be! Snitchy Grass Blabber Mouth is just TOO LONG! How about we combine it all? Snigrablam? Or should it be Snitchblab? I quite like that."

The Abominators looked at Cecil in wonder.

"Listen," said Mucker, "what you did at lunch-time wasn't cool. You grassed us in to Nutter."

"Ah!" said Cecil, understanding at last, "so it's like being a spy: keep your mouth shut and die before telling your secrets?"

"Somethin' like that," said Mucker.

"Well, I'm very sorry," said Cecil. "I will spank myself soundly tonight before I say my prayers. And from this day forth, I will abide by your Code of Secrecy."

"Y"know," said Cheesy, "you're *weird*."

"Thank you," said Cecil. "So is that my nickname? Weirdy Snitch? Snitchy Weird? Or should we stick to Snitchblab?"

Mucker and his gang stood staring at Cecil, as if he was a creature from another planet. Mucker cleared his throat.

"Panty Wanty Weird," he said. The others laughed. Cecil frowned at first, then nodded and smiled, and then his smile widened and turned into a wide grin.

"It's *perfect*," he said. "You're a genius! So does that mean I'm one of your gang?"

Cheesy nudged Mucker, as if to warn him.

"Well, we don't just let anyone join, you know," said Mucker.

"Please can I join? PLEASE? PLEASE!" cried Cecil, dancing up and down in front of Mucker.

Bob made a cut-throat motion with her fingers, and shook her head.

"Nobody can join unless they pass the initiation," said Mucker, looking sideways at his friends, "and that's more or less impossible. So I wouldn't bother if I was you. You don't look strong enough for a start."

"I'm strong!" protested Cecil. "My bodyguard Gustav taught me martial arts, and he used to be an assassin! I'm much stronger than I look! What's the initiation? Tell me!"

Mucker looked at the other Abominators, hoping for some sort of support. Nobody met his eye except Bob, who scowled at him.

"You want to know about the initiation?" said Mucker. "Then meet us by the bike sheds tomorrow. Morning break."

"I'll be there," said Cecil, his eyes shining. "Whatever I need to do, *I'll be ready*."

That night, Cecil and his father discussed their days over another tin of cold baked beans and a radish.

"Well," said Cecil, "the good things were: I am reading the best book I've ever read in my life *and* I am about to join a gang! The bad things were: I accidentally 'grassed' on the Abominators, and apparently hitting someone on the head with your shoe is not how you

make friendy wendies. How about you, Father?"

"Well, Ralph, I went back to the Job Centre, and they sent me down to the Chip Shop, where there was a job frying fish and chips. They showed me how to do everything and then they gave me this apron to wear, and a hair-net and hat for my head."

"That sounds good," said Cecil, encouragingly. But he'd already worked out that things couldn't have gone to plan. Otherwise they'd be eating fish and chips for dinner instead of a dented old tin of baked beans and a radish.

Lord Trumpington-Potts shook his head sadly, a pained expression on his noble face.

"They wanted me to wear a beard-net."

"A *beard*-net?"

"Yes, like a hair-net – only for beards."

"Ah," said Cecil.

"Indeed, young Percy," said Lord-Trumpington-Potts.

They sat in silence for a while, a silence that showed how perfectly they understood each other.

"What shall we do, Father?" said Cecil, after a while.

"How about another game of hide-the-tin-opener?" suggested Lord Trumpington-Potts.

"Hurray!" shouted Cecil. "You go first. I'll count to ten! And *don't* hide it in your beard again."

And so another evening of jollity passed. Cecil and his father might have lost everything except their fine clothes and Cecil's enormous collection of panty wanty woos, but they were splendiferously content.

*

Meanwhile, the Abominators were holding an emergency meeting at Boogster's mum's house. It was their favourite place to meet outside school because Boogster's mum made the best chocolate chip cookies in Grimely. And Boogster had the biggest bedroom.

Mucker had bagged the football-shaped chair, Boogster was sprawled on his bed and Cheesy and Bob were on beanbags.

"OK," said Mucker, through a mouthful of chocolate chip cookie, "let's think of some tasks the little shrimp can't do in a million years."

"Shouldn't be hard," said Bob. "I mean, he's

not got a clue about anything that counts. I bet Panty Wanty Weird couldn't find a toffee in a sweet factory."

"You're always on about sweets," commented Cheesy, "cos your mum won't let you have any, and bakes cakes with sugar substitute."

"At least she doesn't hate noise, like your mum," retorted Bob. "You have to creep round your house in your socks!"

"Stop arguing, you two," said Boogster. "I don't think he's that clueless; he's a brain-box at maths, and he's read Shakespeare and stuff."

"He'll need more than just brains to do our tasks," said Mucker. "He'll need guts."

"Well, we're safe then," said Bob. "I reckon he's gutless. And he can't be strong, or fast. He's so puny."

"You're right," said Cheesy. "Whatever

tasks we think up, we've got nothing to worry about."

*

"There'll be three tasks!" announced Mucker, at the bike sheds the next morning. The gang were lined up with Cecil facing them.

"Why three?" said Cecil. "How about just one?"

"There'll be *three* tasks!" repeated Mucker, more loudly this time. "Unless you pass all of them you can't join the gang. If you're not in the gang, you can't talk to any of us unless you're begging for mercy."

"I've never begged for mercy before," said Cecil. "Is it where you go: 'MERCY! MERCY! I BEG OF YOU! PLEASE, PLEASE DON'T KILL ME, YOU GIANT MURDERER! PLEASE FIND IT IN YOUR EVIL AND DASTARDLY HEART TO SPARE A POOR INNOCENT SOUL LIKE ME!'?"

MERCY! MERCY!
I BEG OF YOU! PLEASE, PLEASE
DON'T KILL ME YOU GIANT
MURDERER!

"Shut your pie hole!" hissed Cheesy. "Mr Coleman's over at the school gate. He'll hear you if you don't put a sock in it."

"Put a sock in it?" Cecil was puzzled. "Where must I put this socky wocky? The same place as the pie?"

"Will you give your mouth a rest and

listen?" said Mucker impatiently. "Do you see the school flagpole? You have to take down the Union Jack and put up a pair of pants *before the bell rings for the end of lunchtime on Monday!*"

"A pair of panty wanty woos? MY panty wanty woos? Up the flagpole?"

"No," said Mucker, his nose wrinkled up in disgust, "not your stinking girlie knickers. You've got to put Nutter's pants up there, see?"

"I see," said Cecil, thoughtfully, "of course. Well, at least I'll have the whole weekend to think up a plan. I hereby accept your challenge! So what are we doing now?"

Mucker and his gang turned and walked away.

"You need to scram, squirt," said Mucker.

"Yeah, hop it!" added Boogster.

"You can't do *nothing* with us unless you're in the gang!" shouted Bob over her shoulder.

Cecil was left, deep in thought, by the bike sheds.

"I need to think of something completely foolproof," he said to himself.

The rest of the day passed uneventfully, apart from when Cecil put his hand up in class and said to Miss Jeffries:

"Can I go potty? I need to make a wee wee and possibly do a poo poo also!"

The Abominators laughed so hard they rolled off their chairs and on to the floor.

"What's so funny?" said Cecil. "It's perfectly natural. Everybody makes wee wees and does poo poos, you know."

Which just made them laugh harder.

It was the weekend. As a special treat, Lord Trumpington-Potts took Cecil to Grimely's Bucket Museum, famous for its collection of buckets from all over the world. There was a Stone Age bucket, made of stone. There was a Bronze Age bucket, made of bronze. There was an Iron Age bucket, made of iron. In a special glass case, with a spotlight shining on it, was a precious jewel-studded Mesopotamian bucket, dated 3000 BC.

MESOPOTAMIAN·BUCKET

Cecil and Lord Trumpington-Potts stared at it for a long time, Cecil scratching his head and Lord Trumpington-Potts scratching his beard.

When they got to the gift shop, Cecil was surprised to see Miss Jeffries behind the counter.

"Hello, Miss Jeffries," he said, "what are *you* doing here?"

"The Bucket Museum is run by volunteers," Miss Jeffries explained with a blush. "I have a passion for the history of buckets, so I help out here on Saturdays."

Lord Trumpington-Potts gazed at Miss

Jeffries. To think that she – like him – had a passion for buckets! He wondered if she also liked camels.

"Are you buying anything, Cecil?" asked Miss Jeffries.

"We can't," he explained, to Lord Trumpington-Potts's embarrassment, "we don't have any money. Not a bean."

"Well, this is from me," said Miss Jeffries, and handed Cecil a notebook with a picture of an Iron Age bucket on the front and a pencil with "I've been to the World-Famous Grimely Bucket Museum" written in gold lettering down the side.

*

That night Cecil worked on his plan. His first idea had been to go to Mr Nutter's house and climb in a window to borrow some of his pants, or perhaps borrow a pair off the washing line.

Unfortunately, Mr Nutter kept his address top secret and was not in the phone book.

So Cecil almost filled his new notebook with notes, diagrams and pictures to help him as he worked out his plan.

There was a picture of Mr Nutter, and a detailed plan of the school with the route marked out between Mr Nutter's office and the flagpole. There were pictures of what Cecil imagined Mr Nutter's pants might look like. And there was a drawing of a monkey, for no particular reason.

"I've got it!" said Cecil, after a long time. "I just need a few things to help me."

He drew pictures of:

1. A white coat
2. A pair of glasses
3. A false moustache

"But where can I find these things?" He lay and racked his brains for ages before the answer came to him. Of course! It was obvious!

He rummaged through his father's enormous trunk of clothes and disguises. Because his father had an outfit for every possible occasion – from flying solo across the

Atlantic to having tea with the Queen – he knew that he would find what he was looking for. And he did.

"Tomorrow," murmured Cecil as he finally got to sleep, "will be a day of triumph for Cecil Trumpington-Potts!"

Cecil's eyes flew open at 6 a.m. on Monday morning. Today was the day, and he knew that he had to get it right. He had to get Mr Nutter's pants up the flagpole, or he would have no chance of joining the Abominators – he'd be finished before he even started.

He was so excited, he could hardly eat his breakfast of four cornflakes and two raisins. This was it. It was time to put his plan into action.

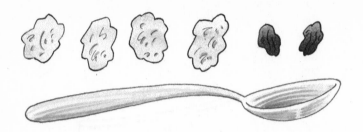

An hour later, Mr Nutter was sitting in his office, not looking forward to the Head Teachers' Conference. It was a three-hour trip, and he just knew that Mr Butter would be on the same early-afternoon train.

He dreaded Mr Butter going on and on about how great Lofty Heights Primary School was and boasting about the school's latest achievement, which was winning one of Grimelyshire's most prized awards: the Shiniest Shoes trophy.

"He'll probably be talking about having to build a new trophy room," thought Mr Nutter bitterly, "because the two rooms they've got already are full. I really hate him! I wish a squirrel would chew off his nose."

At that moment his phone rang.

"Hello," he said, "Nutter here."

"Hello!" said a strange, slightly high-sounding voice on the other end of the line. "Dr Small speaking. I am on my way to my appointment with you."

"What appointment?" Mr Nutter was perplexed.

"I will explain when I get there. I will arrive in exactly five minutes."

Mr Nutter put down the phone and frowned. He was sure that he had not made an appointment with a Dr Small. This was most puzzling.

Five minutes later there was a knock on his door. He opened it to find one of the oddest men he'd ever met standing there. He had thick glasses and a large moustache, and as he was wearing a white coat, which was rather too large for him, Mr Nutter assumed he must be the doctor.

"Dr Small?" he said.

"That is me!" said the tiny doctor, in his high voice.

"So ... why are you here?" Mr Nutter asked, slightly taken aback by having such a very odd-looking doctor appear in his office.

"I am here to inspect your pants," said Dr Small.

There was a long silence. Mr Nutter stared at Dr Small, and Dr Small stared back at Mr Nutter.

"Inspect my pants?" said Mr Nutter, finally.

"Yes. New rules. All head teachers in Grimelyshire must have their pants inspected to ensure that they are wearing appropriate underwear. There have been several cases of head teachers wearing inappropriate underwear, resulting in lack of discipline and general chaos. This order comes directly from the Mayor of Grimely himself, who has very definite ideas about what are the *right* sort of pants."

"But ... "

"Your co-operation is most important," insisted Dr Small. "If you are not helpful in this matter I will have to make a report to the mayor's office. The procedure for pants inspection is as follows:

1. I will leave the room.
2. You will remove your pants and hand them to me through the door so that I can inspect them.
3. I will then return them to you.

Is this understood?"

"Certainly," said Mr Nutter meekly.

*

Standing in his office, about to take off his trousers, Mr Nutter felt puzzled by the appearance of the mysterious Dr Small and this sudden inspection. There was something wrong. There were often inspections, such as the inspection of eyebrow tidiness last year. But there was something about the doctor. Something about his appearance that was not right.

It was not his height; there were plenty of extremely short doctors. His own doctor, Dr Short, was only a metre tall in his platform shoes. And it was not the glasses, or the moustache. So what was it?

The more he thought about it, the more suspicious Mr Nutter got.

"Dr Small, can you come back in here for a moment?" he said.

The strange figure of the doctor re-entered the office, his white coat dragging behind him. Mr Nutter looked at him closely and then saw what was wrong, what had been niggling at the back of his mind. It was the shoes. Gym shoes with a name tape saying "Cecil T-P" glued neatly to the front of them.

Mr Nutter reached forward and yanked at the moustache, which came off in his hand. Then he grabbed at the glasses.

"*Trumpington-Potts!*" he shouted. "I should have guessed! Up to a prank, were you? Well, it didn't work!"

He sat down behind his desk, touching his forehead as if he felt the beginnings of a headache. A terrible Trumpington-Potts-induced headache.

"Mr Butter would never have to put up with this, you know," he said, wearily. "The Lofty Heights Primary children are far too busy winning trophies to play pranks on their head teacher."

Cecil shook his head. "But I didn't

succeed!" he said. "You're *good*, Mr Nutter; you saw right through my disguise. You could be a private detective."

Mr Nutter could not help being slightly pleased with himself. "I suppose that gang put you up to it?" he said.

"Oh no," said Cecil, "it was completely my own idea. But you foiled my plan. I should have realised that you are far too intelligent to fool."

Mr Nutter was so puffed up with pride that he sent Cecil away with just a detention. Cecil walked slowly, his mind racing. If he did not have Mr Nutter's pants soon, he was sunk. It looked as if it was all over, but then again …

"Cecil, we were wondering where you were," said Miss Jeffries, when he walked through the door, still deep in thought. Mucker and his gang looked out of the window, which had a clear view of the flagpole. It was the usual Union Jack flying there. Not Mr Nutter's pants.

"He's not done it!" Bob whispered.

Cecil sat down, his expression unreadable, and opened his notebook. It was time to come up with another plan. He started to scribble furiously.

"You've blown it, haven't you, pipsqueak?" whispered Cheesy. "You've messed up good and proper!" But Cecil was far too deep in thought to answer.

8

The bell went for lunch. The kids in the classroom scrambled towards the door as if their lives depended on it. Cecil remained at his desk. Despite having filled three pages of his notebook, he hadn't thought of another plan. He knew he had to think, and think fast.

Then he remembered something he'd seen in Mr Nutter's office. A train ticket. With today's date on it, and the time of 1 o'clock.

There was something else in Mr Nutter's office. Something very interesting. An overnight bag.

Cecil jumped to his feet.

"Of *course!*" he yelled.

*

"I'm off now, Marjorie!" called Mr Nutter, as he left his office to set off for the station.

Mrs Magpie was busy

going through the lost property box. She'd already found a dirty old oil painting, a porcelain chamber pot, some rubbish and a stuffed badger.

"Righty-ho, Mr Nutter!"

Mr Nutter strode down the corridor, down the stairs and across the playground. The children were filing across it towards the lunch hall. Suddenly, Mr Nutter felt a tugging at his jacket sleeve.

"Trumpington-Potts!" he boomed. "What is it?"

"Sir," said Cecil, "can I carry your bag for you? I'm truly sorry about this morning, Sir. I'd like to make it up to you."

"Hmm, I don't know. It's a large bag, and you're a small boy," said Mr Nutter. "Are you sure you can manage it?"

"Yes, Sir," said Cecil, "I'm stronger than I look. I used to practise wrestling with my pet grizzly bear."

"Don't tell lies, boy!" snapped Mr Nutter, handing Cecil his bag. He strode on, Cecil trotting behind him.

"Mr Nutter," panted Cecil. "What did you mean earlier, about the Lofty Heights Primary children being too busy winning trophies to play pranks?"

Mr Nutter reddened at the very thought of Lofty Heights Primary School.

"They win everything," he said, bitterly. "The shiniest shoes, the best marks, the most perfectly tied ties. They even won the National Most Perfect Primary School trophy last year. Mr Butter is always rubbing my nose in it!"

"That won't do at all, Sir," said Cecil. "I hereby vow, by my father's magnificent beard, that I will do everything I can to win a very large trophy for Grimely East Primary and restore the honour of the school!"

Mr Nutter looked at the strange, skinny boy skipping along beside him. It was difficult to imagine how he could win any sort of trophy for the school.

"Well, I'm sure you will try," he said, kindly.

When they got to the car, Cecil carefully placed the bag in the boot.

"Thank you, Cecil," said Mr Nutter. "I am glad that you are trying to change your ways."

"It's a pleasure, Sir," said Cecil, saluting.

Mr Nutter drove off, humming to himself. It was good that the boy was turning over a new leaf. Perhaps there was hope for him.

Mucker and his gang were already eating jelly and ice cream by the time Cecil sidled into the lunch hall.

"Not hungry? Feeling sick as a parrot?" asked Cheesy.

"Made a honking great mess of things, have you?" added Bob.

"Far from it," said Cecil. "I was wondering if you'd like to accompany me to the playground."

They filed out into the school playground where the Abominators gave a cry of surprise.

A crowd was gathering, including some of the teachers. All were staring at the school flagpole, from which was flying not the Union Jack of an hour before, but a pair of pants. A pair of large, slightly grey pants with loose elastic.

"Look at those grotty old undies!" said Mucker, in wonder. "They *have* to be Nutter's!"

"Are these Mr Nutter's pants?" wondered Mr Coleman. "They look about the right size."

Cecil grinned across at the Abominators, gave them the thumbs up and then walked off whistling to himself.

"Howling kippers! I can't believe he *did* it!" said Bob. "We'll have to make the next task even more difficult."

"Agreed," said Mucker, narrowing his eyes. "There is no way that that girls'-pants-wearing-lunatic is getting into *my* gang!"

*

By the time Mr Nutter reached the room that he and Mr Butter were to share at the Head Teachers' Conference, he had a splitting

headache. He'd had to listen to Mr Butter drone on for the entire train journey about the trophies his school had won that term.

"I wish a dormouse would savage his ankles," Mr Nutter thought.

Both head teachers put their bags on their beds, opened them and began to unpack. Mr Butter was explaining how they'd won the Best Use of Paperclips Trophy when he suddenly stopped talking and stared at Mr Nutter's bag, then raised one eyebrow, and pursed his lips in disapproval.

Mr Nutter glanced down to see what was so interesting. Right at the top of his bag – in full view – were a pair of bright-purple, silk pants with a gold embroidered crest on them.

These were not pants. These were panty wanty woos.

*

"You were lucky, that's all," said Mucker to Cecil at morning break the next day. "Let's see how you do with the next task."

Cecil was munching his way through two apples.

"You hungry?" asked Cheesy. "You're a right grebby guzzler. You don't half go at the free fruit ... have you got none at home?"

The others laughed. Little did Cheesy know just how close to the truth he was. Cecil and his father had nothing to look forward to for dinner that night but the usual baked beans and radishes. But they did not complain. The Trumpington-Potts were made of stern stuff.

"All right," said Mucker. "Here's your next task. You know Lofty Heights Primary up the hill, where the toffee-nosed kids go?"

"Yes," said Cecil, "those kids who win trophies, for being perfect and having the shiniest shoes."

"Funny you should mention the shoes," said Mucker, "seeing as that's exactly what this task is about. The Shiniest Shoes Trophy is the best trophy of all. It's a giant, solid-gold shoe. We want you to bring it to us."

"You mean steal it?" said Cecil. "I can't steal! Stealing is wrong. And bad. And naughty. If I steal something, a big policeman might put me in prison for the *rest of my life*! That would be yucky! And horrid! You have to sleep on a metal bed with no mattress and just one blankie!"

"It's not stealing, wuss-head," said Bob, "it's borrowing. We just want to borrow it for fun, then we'll take it back. Honest."

"Well, if it's *borrowing* I suppose it's OK … " Cecil said. "When do you want it by?"

"Tomorrow morning," said Boogster, "or you fail the initiation!"

"I will deliver it tomorrow," announced Cecil solemnly, and headed back to the school to try to find some more fruit.

"He's got no idea!" said Mucker. "There is no way that daffy dishrag's going to pull this one off. No way!"

*

The first part of Cecil's task involved him finding Lofty Heights Primary School. It would be hard, he reasoned, to borrow the trophy if he didn't actually know where it was.

He rushed home after school, unpacked his rucksack and re-packed it. Cecil had waited his whole life to go on an expedition like his father. He knew exactly what to take with him.

- A long piece of string

- Three safety pins

- A pair of small binoculars

LORD TRUMPINGTON-POTTS

- A compass
- A picture of his father (for inspiration)
- Two radishes

- Spare socks
- Three pairs of panty wanty woos (blue, magenta and daffodil yellow)
- A large stick

He left a note for his father, which said, "On a short expedition. Should be home in time for tea." Then he left the house.

He decided that the name Lofty Heights suggested that the school was at the top of a hill. There was only one hill in the town, so he began to walk towards it.

He saw a lady approaching, so decided to ask her for directions.

"Excuse me, kind-looking old lady," he said. "Would you be able to direct me to Lofty Heights Primary School?"

"I'm not an old lady!" the woman replied, indignantly, "I'm only forty-seven!"

"I hope you don't mind me saying," Cecil said, politely, "but that is positively *ancient* to me!"

"So now you're saying that I'm *ancient?*" asked the woman, beginning to look rather angry.

"I mean that you must have gained great

wisdom from many years of experience," Cecil explained patiently. "You are like a wise old owl!"

"Humph!" exclaimed the lady, walking away.

Cecil was puzzled.

"What did I say?" he called after her.

He chose somebody very different to ask next.

"Excuse me, big and very scary-looking man," he said. "Would you be able to direct me to Lofty Heights Primary School?"

The large man he'd asked looked quite pleased to be called scary.

"Certainly, young gent," he said. "Carry on up the hill and when you get to the police station, turn left. But watch out, or the crocodiles will get you! The posh end of town's full of them. And be careful when you're passing the police station. They'll arrest you for not wearing a top hat!"

He winked, and carried on walking.

"Crocodiles!" said Cecil. "This expedition is becoming very exciting! And why didn't I think of bringing father's top hat? I could go back for it ... no, I don't have time. I'll have to risk it."

He got the large stick out of his rucksack, and as he walked, looked from side to side. He was aware that crocodiles can run faster than humans, and if one came at him he wanted to get a head start.

Soon he found himself approaching the police station. As he drew near, two large policemen came out of the front door.

His heart racing, Cecil leapt behind a post box and

peered around it. The policemen, chatting and laughing, got into their police car and drove off.

Cecil knew he had to get past the entrance to the police station in order to turn left, but what if more policemen came out? He'd be done for.

There was only one thing to do: Cecil ran for it. He hared past the police station, took a left and then he saw it. A large, carved stone building with turrets and stained-glass windows. Lofty Heights Primary School.

Cecil quickly found a side door and began to search for the trophy rooms. Unfortunately the corridors all looked the same, with brown mahogany panelling and thick, expensive red carpets. Cecil was pleased he'd remembered his father's compass.

"I'll head due north," Cecil said to himself, then explore west, south and east."

He found the glass-walled trophy rooms due east. And he did not like what he saw.

The trophies, gleaming like success itself, were protected by a complicated network of laser beams. Worse still, standing outside the doors were two burly security guards with mean looks on their faces. There was no way anyone could get past them.

Cecil was doomed before he even tried.

That night, over the usual baked beans and radishes, Cecil explained his problem to his father, which meant that he had to explain about the initiation.

"I've been initiated a few times myself, Cyril," Lord Trumpington-Potts remembered. "Great fun. Especially the ceremony involving the llama. Well, we can't have you failing, can we? We shall strike tonight! Now, let's look in my trunk. I'm sure I have some robbers' outfits somewhere, from my pyramid-raiding days."

And so it was that at midnight, Cecil and his father were breaking into Lofty Heights Primary School dressed in black-and-white striped robbers' clothes, with black masks covering their eyes, carrying large sacks with 'SWAG' written on them.

"What about the guards and the lasers?" whispered Cecil, as they sidled along a series of corridors.

"Leave that to me, Ralph," said Lord Trumpington-Potts mysteriously.

When they got to the trophy rooms, Cecil and his father found that the security guards were both fast asleep. They were obviously not expecting burglars, because they had brought sleeping bags, cups of cocoa, a big book of bedtime stories and their teddy bears.

"Look, Percy!" said Lord Trumpington-Potts, pointing to the ceiling in one of the trophy rooms. "A trapdoor, and it's right above the Shiniest Shoes Trophy! What luck! Hurry, we need to get to whatever room is above this one."

It did not take them long to find the room above, which was Mr Butter's office. On his desk was a name sign, which read: Mr Roland Butter, B.A. (Hons), Headmaster.

They opened the trapdoor (which was hidden under a rug), and saw below them the Shiniest Shoes Trophy, glistening in the light of all the laser beams and spotlights. It was magnificent.

"There's only one problem," said Lord Trumpington-Potts, rooting around in his SWAG sack, "my special, very strong cat-burglar rope! I *knew* I'd forgotten something!"

"It's OK, Father," said Cecil. "I think I have a solution."

And so it was that Cecil Trumpington-Potts lowered himself into the trophy room, hanging on to his father's specially plaited beard-rope.

"The laser beams!" cried Lord Trumpington-Potts, as his son got close to the trophy. "Be careful!"

Cecil missed a laser beam by a whisker (a whisker of his father's beard to be exact), and managed to grab the giant gold shoe. It was almost too heavy, and for a moment Cecil thought he might drop it, but he managed to hold on as he was pulled to safety.

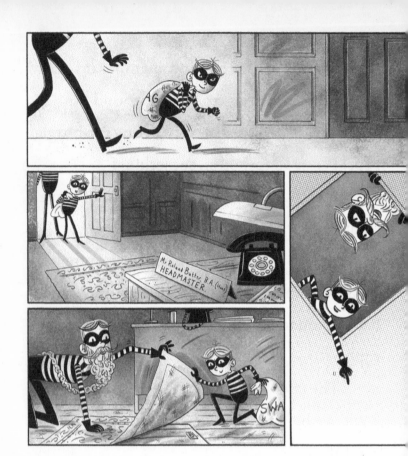

Cecil and his father did a celebration dance around Mr Butter's office, before leaving the security guards a note and making their escape.

You are rubbish Ha! Ha!

The next morning, Cecil led Mucker and his gang to the bike sheds. As he lifted the enormous trophy out of his sack, and it glinted in the sunlight, they gasped and their eyes widened.

"You jammy dodger! That was *impossible!*" muttered Mucker.

"It was an itsy teeny weeny bit hard," admitted Cecil, "but I did it. Now, what's the last task?"

Mucker looked at Cheesy, who looked at Mucker, who looked at Boogster, who looked at Bob, who looked back at Mucker.

They hadn't even thought of a last task, because they'd been so certain that Cecil would not be able to complete the second one.

"WHAT IS THIS?" boomed a voice behind

them. It was Mr Nutter, and his face was purple with rage. Cecil was still holding the trophy.

"It's the Shiniest Shoes Trophy, Sir," he said, smiling proudly.

Mucker groaned. "He's only about to give the game away!" he whispered to Cheesy.

"And WHAT are you doing with that trophy, Trumpington-Potts?" thundered Mr Nutter.

"I was just about to take it back to Lofty Heights Primary, Sir," said Cecil innocently. "You see, I've just opened this sack. In this sack is this trophy, which has obviously been stolen by thieves … or perhaps borrowed. It must be returned immediately."

Mr Nutter looked impressed. "Well done, boy!" he said. "Good work! Do you know, I think I'll take it back to them myself. I'll tell Mr Butter to be more careful next time."

He took the trophy from Cecil and strode off with a spring in his step.

"How did you get away with that?" Mucker was amazed. "He *believed* you! He's never believed us."

"It must be the well posh way he talks, and that he doesn't look all shifty-eyed the way you do when you tell a whopper," said Cheesy.

"I didn't lie, actually," said Cecil. "Everything I said was true. I just left out a few minor details, that's all. Now what is the final task?"

"We'll have to think about that," said Mucker. "We'll tell you after school."

*

At lunchtime, the Abominators met in their Top-Secret Gang Headquarters. The mood was serious.

"This is bad. We've got to think of something he can NEVER achieve," said Mucker, pacing up and down, "not in a million years."

"But what if he does it?" Cheesy said. "He's done the other two tasks, and who'd have thought he could? He's … not human, he's not. He must have special powers."

"Listen, even if he does a hundred tasks, he's not getting in," said Bob, "or I'm leaving. He's even more bonkers than my Auntie Flora. And she wears a colander on her head!"

"Mucker, you've got to promise you won't let him in," added Boogster, "or there won't be a gang. We mean it."

"OK," said Mucker. "Even if he manages it I'll tell him he still can't join. I give you my

solemn vow. Anyway, it might not come to that. I think I've thought of something that nobody could do."

"What?" asked Bob.

"Nobody could beat Lofty Heights Primary's record for selling the most strawberries on Grimelyshire Strawberry-Selling Day, could they?"

Booster grinned.

"You're right! That record's unbeatable! It was set twenty years ago, and nobody's managed it since."

"Mucker," said Bob. "You're a genius!"

*

After school, the gang told Cecil about his next task.

"Strawberry-Selling Day?" he said. "Interesting! I will need to do some serious planning."

"You'd better get on with it," said Cheesy. "It's next week!"

"Then I don't have a minute to waste!" cried Cecil.

Cecil skipped off, his face glowing with happiness. The gang watched him go. There was a long silence.

"You know what?" said Mucker, in a puzzled voice.

"What?" said Bob.

"I feel ... sort of bad about this."

Boogster shuffled his feet. "Me too," he said.

"And me," said Cheesy.

Bob sniffed. "You're all going soft," she said. But she didn't sound very convincing.

At home, Cecil found Lord Trumpington-Potts in an extremely gloomy mood.

"Today they sent me out street sweeping," he explained to Cecil. "People were dropping rubbish on the ground behind me, littering where I'd just swept. I marched a teenager to a rubbish bin to dispose of his burger wrapper but apparently that's 'common assault'. My supervisor said I was lucky they didn't call the police!"

Cecil was not unhappy like his father; he was very happy. He was starting to think about his next task.

"Father," he announced, "I have to go to the library. I have to find out about selling. And I also have to find out about strawberries."

"Cecil," said Lord Trumpington-Potts, "you are an inspiration. You set your mind to something, and you achieve it!"

"You called me Cecil!" said Cecil, his mouth open in amazement.

"Of course I did," said his father. "That is your name, isn't it? Well, Cecil, your dedication and determination remind me of your great great great uncle Cosmo. He decided to build a replica of the leaning tower of Pisa in the grounds of his manor house, to please his third wife, who was Italian. Everybody told him that he would never succeed, but he didn't listen. He said he could do it, and by jove he did it! It took ten years to complete and great great great uncle Cosmo spent most of his fortune on it. In fact, he was so obsessed with the project, his wife left him and went back to Italy. But when it was finished it was a *triumph*!"

Cecil's eyes shone.

"Can you take me to see it one day, Father?"

Lord Trumpington-Potts cleared his throat.

"I'm afraid not, dear boy," he said. "The great hurricane of 1824 knocked it over. It was leaning too far, apparently. It landed on poor old Cosmo. Terrible business. Now let's go to the library!"

So they went to the library, where Cecil found a book about selling called: *How to Sell Anything, Including Strawberries* and a book called: *Strawberries: The Facts.*

"Interesting," he said as he pored over the books, "*very* interesting!"

Meanwhile, Lord Trumpington-Potts read a book titled "Beard Maintenance on a Budget". It was a very successful visit.

On the way home, Cecil asked if they could go into the fruit shop where he persuaded the shop owner to give him a huge bundle of brown paper bags for free.

"What are they for?" asked Lord Trumpington-Potts.

"All part of the plan, Father," said Cecil, mysteriously, "all part of the plan!"

*

At assembly on National Strawberry-Selling Day Mr Nutter was in a surprisingly good mood. He'd really enjoyed wiping the smug look off Mr Butter's face the previous week, when he waved the Shiniest Shoes Trophy in his face.

Also, Cecil Trumpington-Potts had marched into his office the day before and announced that he was going to beat Lofty Heights Primary's strawberry-selling record. And from the determined look on the boy's face, he believed him. Things were beginning to look up.

"Good luck, boys and girls," he said. "May the contest begin! You have until noon!"

*

Cecil queued to collect his first punnets of strawberries, alongside the Abominators. Most children had wicker baskets to fill, but Cecil was wheeling a large wheelbarrow, which he'd borrowed from Miss Jeffries.

"You think you can sell a whole barrow load?" asked Cheesy.

"I KNOW I can!" said Cecil, confidently.

The Abominators looked tired. None of them had slept well the night before. All had been plagued with feelings of guilt about Cecil. Even Bob.

"Listen," said Mucker, who couldn't bear it any longer, "we'd better tell you something."

"What?" said Cecil.

"We've only given you the tasks so you'll fail them and we won't have to let you join the gang. We don't want you in it, see?"

Cecil looked at them in disbelief.

"So you've been setting me all these tasks, and you were NEVER going to let me join?" he said.

The Abominators all nodded, looking at the floor. They couldn't meet his eye.

"So … why are you telling me now?" asked Cecil.

Boogster cleared his throat.

"Because this last task, it's impossible. I suppose we don't want you to bust a gut trying to do it when we know we're not going to let you join. We're beginning to feel … bad about it all."

Cecil stared at them.

"You're *beginning to feel bad*?" he repeated.

"Yes," said Mucker, looking uncomfortable.

Cecil began to smile. And then his smile turned into a massive grin.

"Well, you know what *that* means, don't you?"

"What?" said Cheesy.

"It means that you must *like me*!"

"No we don't!" said Bob. "You're a la-di-da lunatic!"

Cecil kept grinning.

"Oh yes you do!"

"We don't like you," said Mucker emphatically, "because you wear girly pants and you talk like a baby and you're *weird*."

"You CARE ABOUT ME!" shouted Cecil,

ecstatic, as he danced a little dance of joy, in a circle around the Abominators. "Oh yes you do! You felt bad, and that shows you CARE. This must be the happiest day of my life. I have friends, and they LIKE me!"

Mucker and his gang collected their strawberries, and headed off in different directions.

"You're not in the gang," Boogster shouted over his shoulder, "OK? So you don't have to sell the most strawberries, all right? You're not going to get in the gang, *no matter what*."

Cecil stood and let them go, still smiling.

"They *like* me," he said to himself, happily.

*

Cheesy went to the posh end of Grimely, hoping that people would have more money to buy strawberries. At the first house, a man answered the door and called to his wife:

"Petunia, there's a small undernourished boy who looks rather like a mouse selling strawberries. Shall I tell him to go away?"

"Tell him we only buy from Lofty Heights children!" she trilled from the kitchen.

Boogster and Mucker tried the train station, where Boogster did some breakdancing to try to attract customers.

"I'm not buying from *you!*" one man said to Mucker, who was holding the basket of strawberries. "Your fingernails are filthy, and it looks as if you've not washed behind your ears for at least two years! You are unhygienic!"

*

Cecil did not go knocking on doors selling like the others; he went straight to the town square in the very centre of Grimely. He parked his wheelbarrow, and started to shout:

"FREE strawberries! Get your FREE strawberries here!"

Soon an enormous queue had formed, because there is nothing that people like better than free stuff.

The first person in the queue – a lady wearing a large hat – watched as Cecil filled one of his brown paper bags with strawberries.

"That will be fifty pence, please," said Cecil, holding out his hand.

"I thought they were free!" said the lady, indignantly.

"They are," said Cecil, "but the bag costs fifty pence. Can I just point out how very juicy and delicious these strawberries are?"

"Oh, all right," said the lady, whose mouth was watering at the sight of the delicious fruit.

She took the paper bag of strawberries, putting a shiny fifty pence coin into Cecil's outstretched hand.

The same thing happened with the next customer, and the next. Everybody was slightly annoyed that they had to pay for the bag, but paid their fifty pence anyway when they saw how tasty the strawberries looked. Soon Cecil had sold out, and had to run back to the school to refill his wheelbarrow – several times.

*

Bob was in a bad mood. She hadn't enjoyed feeling guilty about what they'd done. She blamed Cecil.

"He's as mad as a howling kipper!" she muttered to herself. "And he's a girly toff!"

She was so annoyed with Cecil and herself, she was tempted to just go home and get her mum to pay her for her strawberries. But she knew that her mum would then insist on making strawberry tarts with her, and make her wear a frilly apron. Bob could think of nothing worse. So she followed her original plan and headed towards the hospital. Her idea was that people who were visiting sick people might buy some strawberries.

Bob stood outside the front entrance to Casualty. She put her basket of strawberries on the ground, and held up her homemade sign, which she had written on two sides of an old cardboard box. It had taken her ages the night before and she was quite proud of it. It said: TASTEEIST STROBERYZS EVER!! GOOD FOR SICK PEEPLE!

Spelling was not Bob's strong point.

Ten minutes passed, but nobody stopped.

Then a girl from Lofty Heights Primary turned up, in her smart blazer and very shiny shoes, with not a hair out of place. She calmly put up a small table, and laid out her punnets of strawberries perfectly. She had a professional-looking sign which said: DELICIOUS, SCRUMMY STRAWBERRIES! A PERFECT PRESENT FOR SOMEONE IN HOSPITAL!

Delicious, Scrummy STRAWBERRIES! A Perfect present for someone in hospital! x

The Lofty Heights girl looked across at Bob, with her badly spelt sign, and sniffed in a superior way.

Lots of children were, like the Abominators, finding it hard to sell their strawberries. And as the morning went on, everybody they asked said the same thing.

"No thanks," people said, "we're going to the town centre; someone's giving them away for free there!"

By the end of the morning, Cecil had sold over a hundred punnets of strawberries. But was that enough to restore the honour of Grimely East Primary?

At assembly the next day, Mr Nutter was beside himself with excitement. On the podium in front of him was a giant, shiny trophy in the shape of a strawberry.

Standing at the back of the hall, not sure what to think of it all, were Mucker and his gang.

"He *did it*," said Boogster. "He only went and did it, didn't he?"

"This is a turning point in the history of Grimely East Primary!" Mr Nutter cried. "It's all thanks to one boy for helping us beat Lofty Heights Primary in *something* for the first time in history. Three cheers for Cecil Trumpington-Potts!"

There was a resounding silence.

For about three seconds.

And then there was the most enormous cheer you've ever heard in your life. People were whooping and hollering and stamping their feet.

Mucker and his gang did not join in.

At first.

But then they couldn't help it; they started cheering like everybody else, and Bob did her loud whistle where she put her fingers in the sides of her mouth.

It was Mucker himself that led the cry:
"Ce-cil! Ce-cil! Ce-cil!"

And Miss Jeffries shouted: "Speech!"

So Cecil went up on to the stage of the

assembly hall and waited for the cheers to die down, which took some time. Then he spoke.

"Ladies and gentlemen. Boys and girls. It is a great honour to be standing before you today with this shiny trophy. We've been losing to Lofty Heights Primary for too long! Today I swear, by my father's beard and by every pair of panty wanty woos that I own, that we'll beat them in lots of other things too! Because WE RULE!"

Bob jumped up.

"Yes, he's right! WE RULE!" she shouted, thinking about the self-satisfied girl from Lofty Heights Primary who'd sniffed at her. "We TOTALLY rule!"

"Hurrah!" everybody shouted, cheering even louder than before.

Cecil climbed off the stage and walked through the crowd, straight over to the Abominators.

"Well," he said, "I did it, didn't I? But don't worry, I know you still don't want me in the gang."

Mucker looked at Bob. Bob looked at Boogster. Boogster looked at Cheesy. Cheesy looked at Mucker. In other words they were all looking at each other.

"It's up to you, Bob," said Mucker. "You're the one who's most against the idea."

Bob frowned. This was not going to plan, not at all. But then she looked at the giant trophy, the first they'd ever won, and the happy pupils, and finally at Cecil's scrubbed, shining, hopeful face.

"You can be an Associate Member," she said at last. "It's NOT a proper member, OK? You can't come to the Top Secret Meetings or nothing, or to Boogster's mum's house. But you can sort of... *associate* with us now and again."

"ASSOCIATE MEMBER?" cried Cecil. "Would you REALLY let me be one?"

Mucker nodded.

"I reckon," he said.

Boogster grinned. Cheesy slapped Cecil on the back. Mucker shook Cecil's hand solemnly. Bob wondered what she'd just agreed to.

Cecil jumped up and down, like a mad grasshopper.

"I'm IN THE GANG!" he shouted. "I can't believe it! I've actually got friends! This is the happiest day of my life."

"You're NOT in the gang!" said Bob. "Didn't you hear me? You're just an associate member."

But Cecil wasn't listening.

"Hip, hip, hooray! I'm jumping for joy! Look at me! LOOK AT ME!!!"

Mucker groaned, "Cecil," he said, "please stop jumping. It *ain't cool*."

"You're right," said Cecil, stopping. "I'm boiling my little botty wotty off."

"What are we going to *do* with him?" whispered Bob to Mucker, as they all filed off to the classroom. "I think we might have just made a BIG mistake."

"Maybe we have," said Mucker, "but I can tell you one thing. From now on it's not going to be dull round here."

And so it was that Cecil Trumpington-Potts at last found some friends. And despite being the poorest boy in all of Grimely, Cecil was happier than he'd ever been in his whole, entire life.

Find more mischief, mess
and mayhem in:

About The Author

J. L. Smith lives in Buckinghamshire with a delinquent partner, several delinquent children and a delinquent dog.

J. L. Smith enjoys many hobbies including crisp eating, midnight trampolining and hiding in wardrobes, and has been known to laugh for over twenty minutes when shown a picture of a dog wearing sunglasses.

If stranded on a desert island, J. L. Smith's luxury item would be a large wheel of cheese.